In Memory of Michael Murphy
– *M.C.*

For Mom & Dad
– *G.W.*

First published in the United States 1996 by
Little Tiger Press,
12221 West Feerick Street, Wauwatosa, WI 53222
Originally published in Great Britain 1994 by
Magi Publications, London
Text © 1994 Michael Coleman
Illustrations © 1994 Gwyneth Williamson
CIP Data is available.
All rights reserved.
Printed in Italy
First American Edition
ISBN 1-888444-02-9
1 3 5 7 9 10 8 6 4 2

# LAZY OZZIE

*by*
## Michael Coleman

*Pictures by*
## Gwyneth Williamson

Ozzie was a very lazy owl.

"It's time you learned to fly," said Mother Owl one day.

But Ozzie said, "Oh, do I have to?"

He didn't want to learn to fly. All that wing-flapping looked like too much hard work. Ozzie's favorite thing to do was to sit around.

"I'm practicing being wise," he said.

"Well, I want you to fly,"
said his mother sternly.
"Now, I'm going out to look
for some food. And if you *are* wise,
you will be on the ground by the time I come back!"

Ozzie thought hard.

If he was wise, then he should be able to
think of a way of getting down to the
ground without flying.

Suddenly he noticed the horse who lived
in their barn. The horse's head came up
almost as high as the beam Ozzie
was sitting on.

Ozzie had an idea . . .

"Help, help!" he yelled.
"What's the matter?" asked the
high horse.

"It's an emergency!" cried Ozzie, jumping onto
the high horse's back. "Take me to the milk shed!"

So the high horse
took Ozzie to the milk shed.

In the milk shed there lived a cow who wasn't quite
as high as the high horse.

"It's an emergency!" cried Ozzie, jumping
onto the not-quite-so-high cow's back.
"Take me to the pigsty!"

So the high horse and the not-quite-so-high cow took Ozzie to the pigsty.

In the pigsty there lived a pig. The pig wasn't as tall as the not-quite-so-high cow. But he was a big pig. "It's an emergency!" cried Ozzie, jumping onto the big pig's back. "Take me to the barnyard!"

So the high horse,
the not-quite-so-high cow
and the big pig took Ozzie
to the barnyard.

In the barnyard there lived a sheepdog.
The sheepdog wasn't as tall as the big pig.
He was a short sheepdog.
"It's an emergency!" cried Ozzie, jumping
onto the short sheepdog's back.
"Take me to the pasture!"

So the high horse, the not-quite-so-high cow, the big pig and the short sheepdog took Ozzie to the pasture.

In the pasture there lived a lamb. The lamb wasn't as tall as the short sheepdog. She was a little lamb. "It's an emergency!" cried Ozzie, jumping onto the little lamb's back.

"Take me to the duck pond!"

So the high horse, the not-quite-so-high cow, the big pig, the short sheepdog and the little lamb took Ozzie to the duck pond.

In the duck pond there lived a duck. The duck wasn't as tall as the little lamb. He was a dinky duck. "It's an emergency!" cried Ozzie, jumping onto the dinky duck's back. "Take me to the barn!"

So the high horse, the not-quite-so-high cow,
the big pig, the short sheepdog,
the little lamb and the dinky duck
took Ozzie back to the barn.

As soon as they got there, Ozzie hopped down
to the ground from the dinky duck's back.
He'd done it!
Now that's what you call being wise,
he told himself!

"So what's the emergency?" asked the high horse.
"Oh," said Ozzie. "I was only kidding. Wasn't that fun?"

The high horse, the not-quite-so-high cow, the big pig, the short sheepdog, the little lamb and the dinky duck weren't amused.

They went away grumbling.

But Ozzie was happy. His plan had worked.

He was pretty wise already.

"I flew all the way down,"
he said proudly to his mother
when she came back.

Mother Owl gave him a big smile.
"That's wonderful," she said.
Ozzie thought she was
pleased with him . . .

. . . but he didn't know
that she'd been watching
the whole time.
"Now let me see you fly
back up again,"
said Mother Owl.

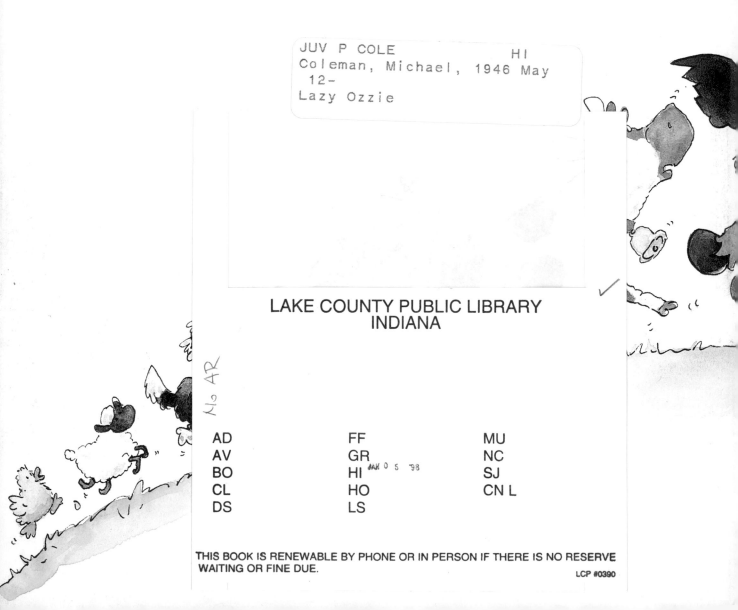